IT'S INCREDIBLE !

YOU WONT BELEIVE IT !!!

IT'S AN ADVENTURE !

CASHIER AND ROGER

By Jolimichel Robinson
& illustrated by Ron Cunnigham

AuthorHouse™
1663 Liberty Drive
Bloomington, IN 47403
www.authorhouse.com
Phone: 1 (800) 839-8640

Published by AuthorHouse 05/23/2019

ISBN: 978-1-7283-1339-9 (sc)
ISBN: 978-1-7283-1338-2 (e)

Library of Congress Control Number: 2019942697

Print information available on the last page.

This book is printed on acid-free paper.

authorHOUSE®

Printed in the United States
By Bookmasters